Tallulah's

Flying Adventure

Printed in the United States of America
by Crooked Tail Press

First Printing, 2016

ISBN: 978-1-946380-00-5
Ebook ISBN: 978-1-946380-01-2

A fable with an ancient feel, this story of a plucky spider and her tiny bird companion rests comfortably in the story-telling tradition of Native American peoples.

This is a book for children that people of all ages can appreciate for its multi-layered charms. There are simple but endearing pen and ink illustrations, and every chapter begins with a quotation from Native American lore, such as this, from the Wisdom of the Elders: "We are each a thread in the web of life, strengthened by the promise of our dreams." The story itself has many symbols and harks back to a simpler time when children learned such natural but surprisingly mature themes from their elders. Tallulah embodies many admirable qualities, making her a role model of bravery and persistence, while Buck and the bird represent friendship and loyalty. The book offers a small list of Lakota words interspersed in the narrative. Thus, it offers many ways to learn.

Story-telling springs naturally from her background, allowing her to create, in Tallulah's Flying Adventure, a tale ideal for reading aloud and sure to engage the reader as much as the listener.

Chanticleer Book Reviews

Gloria Two-Feathers is a wonderful new voice in the realm of children's stories. But Tallulah's Flying Adventure should not be limited to just children. The author's lyrical voice begs for this story to be read out loud, and within the tale readers young and old will hear the underlying music that propels the adventure forward. This is a story of Tallulah learning who she is, realizing her strengths, and discovering the importance of not just friendships but more importantly, of loyalty and love. All of this is told within an adventure that will cause any child reading, or hearing, to immediately sail away in their imaginations to join Tallulah. I hope to hear more from this author.

Lisa Stowe, author of the Mountain Mystery Series

Tallulah's Flying Adventure by Gloria Two-Feathers is a charming story of a unique spider and her big heart. This story reminds me of Aesops Fables in the way it's told and the lesson it presents. Good, strong writing from Two-Feathers here, that children will enjoy. I can't wait to read more from this author.

Sharon E Anderson, award-winning author, Development Outreach at Chanticleer Reviews, President of Skagit Valley Writers League

Tallulah's Flying Adventure by Gloria Two Feathers should join the ranks of books like The Giving Tree by Shel Silverstein, Old Turtle by Douglas Wood and The Runaway Bunny by Margaret Wise Brown--books that communicate far more than what is on the printed page. Like those books, Tallulah's Flying Adventure teaches affirming life lessons with gentle grave and heartfelt wisdom.

It provides an introduction to Native American spirituality that is both entertaining and thought provoking.
Filled with images of spinning and weaving, it points the way to spinning connections between us and the spirit world, between us and the natural world and between us and others.

The Pronunciation Guide in the back of the book is helpful.

A useful book for teachers, Scout leaders, and spiritual teachers of all stripes. Perhaps it's greatest value will be to parents and grandparents who will use it to help the children in their lives discover their place in our complicated and beautiful world.

Elizabeth Ellis, awarded Master Storyteller, National Storytelling Network Lifetime Achievement Recipient and author of, *From Plot to Narrative* and *Calling in the Wolf*

Between the covers of this delightful book you'll find a mystical story about a friendship between a horse and a spider and a bird. A beautiful spider with a warrior's heart sets out on a journey to seek the answer to a dire problem. An adventure of bravery and tenacity. Along the way, you'll be introduced to Native American origin beliefs and some of the language that envelopes it. Gloria Two Feathers brings to life the healing power of friendship.

AJ Kiffe, Author, Microbiologist, Mom

A story of friendship, an incredible quest, and learning of one's personal strengths. We all have to make unforeseen journeys in our lives, journeys that seem impossible. Yet with helpers and true friends, we grow and can make it through.

The elements of Native American spirituality woven all through Tallulah's quest and her life remind and connect the reader to the Earth, the elements, and their own spirit. Each of us is intrinsic to the natural world around us.

Tallulah, Buck, and Bird Friend are a triumphant trio, unique individuals with different skills and strengths.
A wonderful story to read again and again.

Mary Dessein, Writer, Musician, Radio Host

Table of Contents

Chapter One: Mother Spider's Cocoon   p. 1

Chapter Two: Keeper of the Meadow   p. 9

Chapter Three: Magical Bird   p. 17

Chapter Four: Flight   p. 25

Chapter Five: Up, Up, Up!   P. 35

Chapter Six: The Rescue   p. 43

Chapter even: Friend to the Rescue   p. 49

Chapter Eight: Elixir of Life   p. 55

Chapter Nine: Gratitude   p. 63

What is good in this book

is given back to the Earth

and all her children.

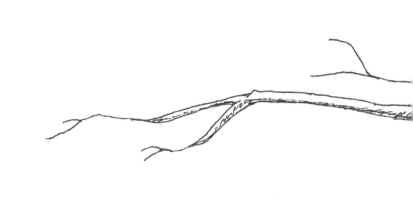

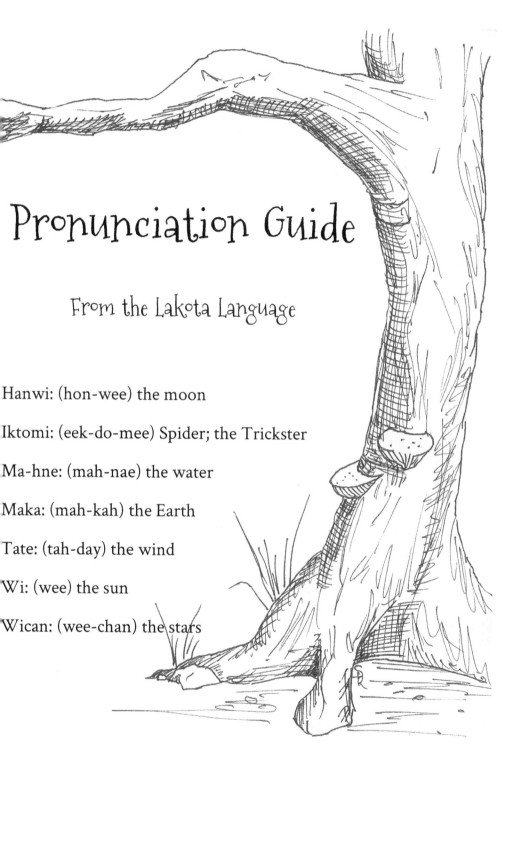

Pronunciation Guide

From the Lakota Language

Hanwi: (hon-wee) the moon

Iktomi: (eek-do-mee) Spider; the Trickster

Ma-hne: (mah-nae) the water

Maka: (mah-kah) the Earth

Tate: (tah-day) the wind

Wi: (wee) the sun

Wican: (wee-chan) the stars

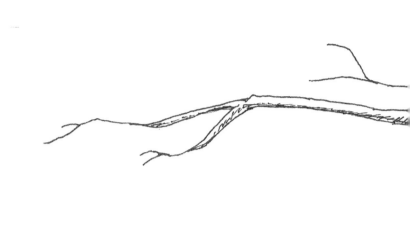

Chapter I

Mother Spider's Cocoon

Grown men can learn from very little children,

for the hearts of little children are pure.

Therefore, the Great Spirit may show them

many things which older people miss.

Black Elk, Lakota Holy Man

I would like to tell you the story of Iktomi the Spider a Trickster Spirit. His Medicine is to teach us lessons. The lessons he teaches are not harmful but difficult nevertheless. He is a Sacred Being, but he has too many flaws to be perfect. Doesn't this sound a little bit like us? In spite of his flaws he has another side to his Medicine. Iktomi the Spider can be a Healer, too. Throughout time one of his descendants became just that, a Healer. And this is her incredible story.

~ ~ ~ ~ ~

It begins in a place that is between up and down in a distant magical land unknown to most of us. But nevertheless, it is right under our noses.

In this place there lived a Mother Spider. She laid hundreds of eggs and wound them tight into a beautiful cocoon that would protect them from the cold and wind. She chose the perfect place to lay her eggs-under the eaves of an old barn, which stood beside a lush green meadow, teaming with life. The sweet fragrance of grass, flowers, and trees filled the air and across the meadow was a flourishing old forest full of birds, butterflies, and all kinds of forest creatures.

The Mother Spider kept watch over her eggs, waiting for them to hatch. She gently stroked the cocoon with her long slender legs, while she sang an ancient song, "Ah ne ya, ah ne ya, ah ne yen," until at last there was a great commotion in the cocoon and the eggs opened. One by one the baby spiders emerged. They were so small and tiny they looked like little black dots.

As in the many generations before and the many

generations to come it was the custom of the spiders that as

soon as all the babies were strong

enough they would leave the web to make their way in the

world and create their own homes. After which the

Mother Spider would join her ancestors in the Spirit world.

Once the Mother Spider had kissed each one and sent them on their way, she noticed one last egg had not hatched. *How unusual*, the Mother Spider thought. She listened very closely, as she thought she heard something in the egg stir. Yes, there it was again; she had heard it.

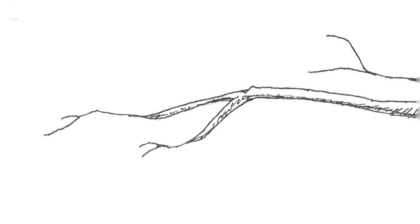

Chapter 2

Keeper of the Meadow

All the days of your life...

May you walk gently through

the world and know it's beauty

Native American Wisdom

So the Mother Spider continued singing her ancient song, "Ah ne ah, ah ne ah, ah ne yen." She stroked and stroked and rolled the egg with her long slender legs. It seemed quite a long time. She was sure the sun had rose and set twice and the moon was getting larger, before there was a commotion in the egg. The silken threads of the cocoon began to separate and one tiny leg appeared followed by the baby spider.

She looked very different from her sisters and brothers, as they were teeny tiny and all black. But she was pure white with golden eyes and soft golden hair on her long slender legs.

The Mother Spider kissed her and was sending her out to find her way in the world,

when the young spider looking around said, "I like this place, I will live right here."

The young spider was very curious as she began to look about. The old barn was enormous compared to the young spider, but she had great courage and a warrior's heart, so off she went to explore her new home. She had a good sense of smell and noticed the fragrance of fresh hay, old wood, and other pleasant scents left by those who had previously lived there.

It wasn't very long before she discovered that an old horse lived in a stall in the barn.

The horse was very friendly and greeted her with a neigh, saying, "Hello my name is Buck, and I'm the Keeper of the Meadow. I don't ever recall seeing a spider that looked quite like you do. What is your name?"

The young spider said she did not have a name.

"You are so unique looking, I'm going to give you a special name," Buck said. "I'm going to name you, Tallulah."

Buck and Tallulah became great friends and he invited her to live in his stall with him. Every day Buck would go out to the Meadow to graze. And every evening he returned smelling of fresh air, sunshine, and sweet grass.

He enjoyed the company of his new friend and he told her many things about the world outside the Old Barn.

He told her about Wi the Sun, Hanwi the Moon, and Tate the Wind; Ma-hne the Water and the Standing Nation, the Trees. And he told her of the Great Grandmother Tree who was the Tree of Life and stood at the heart of the Old Forest. He told her much about the world of the plants and the Winged Nation, the Birds, and other magical creatures he had seen in his long life.

Tallulah was amazed to hear about the world outside the Old Barn. Her favorite stories were about the Winged Nation and flying.

One evening Buck told Tallulah a special story of another great weaver of webs, the wise old Great Grandmother Spider.

"It was told," Buck said "that she was here in the beginning of time and she had helped in the creation of the Universe. It was the Great Spirit who ask her to spin a web that would unite and hold the universe together. And to this very day it still keeps all of creation connected."

When Buck would go out to the Meadow to graze, Tallulah would practice spinning and building webs in the eaves. All the while she daydreamed of flying through the air like a bird.

Chapter 3

Magical Bird

Oh, Great Spirit

Hear me, I am small and weak,

I need your strength and wisdom.

Chief Yellow Lark, Lakota

One day Buck didn't go out to the Meadow, or the next day, or the day after that. He became very quiet and then fell into a deep sleep.

A grey mist crept across the Meadow and all of nature fell silent.

Tallulah was very concerned for her dear friend. She knew he was sick, but didn't know what to do for him. She quickly spun a silken thread and lowered herself down beside him. She stroked his dull hair with her long slender legs and sang him an ancient song, but he did not stir.

Then she began to pray. She said a prayer of help, health, and happiness for her old friend. She thought, *If only I could go to the Old Forest, to the Great Grandmother Tree, she would know how to help. But my legs are too short to make a journey like that. I wish I could fly.*

Right at that moment she heard a great ruckus in one of her webs under the eaves. Tallulah quickly climbed up on one of her invisible threads to the web. What she saw made her pause and back up a little on the quivering thread. There tangled in her web was the smallest of birds. He was the size of a moth. He was brilliantly colored with iridescent feathers of blue and green, with a yellow beak and legs.

He looked like a magical bird.

Lifting her two front legs so she could feel the air for any signs of danger, she approached him slowly.

"Please don't eat me," he pleaded in a shaky voice. "I'm so small and skinny I wouldn't make much of a meal for you. Please set me free and let me fly again."

Tallulah was so surprised, she just sat and looked at him. Many birds had flown through the Old Barn. But she had never seen one this small and so brightly colored, and she didn't know birds could talk.

Once again he pleaded for his life. "Please let me go. If you let me go I can tell you how you can fly."

Jumping up and down Tallulah said, "Fly? Me! Yes, yes please."

Tallulah explained to the magical little bird about what had happened to Buck and how she wanted to help him. She told him if she could fly she would go to the Great Grandmother Tree for help. When she was finished, she said, "If I let you go do you promise not to fly away? And do you promise you will tell me how I can fly?"

"Oh yes, yes I promise you anything you want. Just please release me from your web," pleaded the little bird.

Using her many legs Tallulah quickly untangled all the silvery threads that bound the little bird. As soon as he was free he flew to the nearest rafter in the barn. He was so happy he beat his tiny little wings and sang a joyful song.

"Now keep your promise and tell me how I can fly," said Tallulah.

The beautiful little bird said, "You are a very skillful spinner. Tonight there is the most special of all moons rising. In the light of this sacred blood red moon, spin your strongest and finest web. Make sure it's woven with care.

For it is a long way to the Great Grandmother Tree."

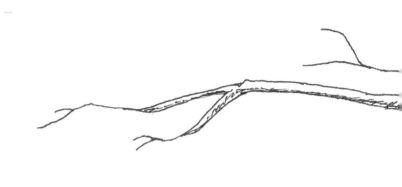

Chapter 4

Flight

We are each a thread in

the web of life, strengthened

by the promise of our dreams

Wisdom of the Elders

All through the night under the pale light of Hanwi the Moon, Tallulah spun the best web she had ever made. When she was finished she anchored it down by a pool of dew and waited.

Just when Wi the Sun began his journey across the morning sky, his companion, Tate the Wind blew soft and warm as a breath. A shiver of excitement ran through her; Tallulah kicked off the dewdrops that had gathered on her web. And with a mighty leap off the Old Barn she launched herself and her web into the air. The web was just like a great sail on a ship. With the little bird flying along with her, she found that by shifting her weight on each of her eight legs, she could steer her web through the air.

She was so amazed and delighted she shouted. "I'm flying, I'm flying! And I'm off on a great adventure!"

"Since you have such great courage, a kind heart, and you saved my life, I will go with you," the little bird said as he flew beside her. "Follow me and I will guide you to the Great Grandmother Tree. I know someone there who may be able to help us."

The grey mist was thickening, filling the Meadow below. Tallulah felt grateful she sailed high enough to be above the menacing fog.

Even though it was a long way across the Meadow, flying helped them arrive very quickly to the edge of the Old Forest. With little Bird Friend guiding the way, she was able to steer her web-sail around and through the Standing Nation, the Trees, until she was deep in the heart of the Old Forest. The tall trees filtered out the bright sunlight, creating cool shadows. Gazing through the shadows Tallulah saw a soft glowing light. Sensing this was what she was looking for she followed the inviting glow.

Entering into a large clearing she was amazed at what she saw. It took her breath away. The sun was streaming its golden light down on a huge old gnarled tree that stood so tall Tallulah couldn't see the top of it. It was as wide as it was tall, with branches the size of large tree trunks. Its leaves were as big as Hanwi the Moon when she was full.

Tallulah could feel the powerful life force she cast out in all directions. The ancient Great Grandmother Tree was beautiful.

Tallulah sailed around and around through the Great Grandmother Tree's very large branches. Feeling puzzled she thought, *Now that I'm here, I'm not sure what to do.*

Just then Bird Friend shouted, "There she is, the one I thought would be able to help us." Sitting in very large web that was anchored between two of the enormous branches was the Grandmother Spider.

"I thought it was a story and she was a myth," Tallulah gasped to her friend. With a feeling of awe she said, "But she is real."

Tallulah felt shy and a little afraid in her presence. But she remembered her friend Buck and she found the courage to speak.

Taking a deep breath, with a shaky voice Tallulah called out to her, "Grandmother, we need your help. We have traveled a long way. Will you please help us?"

Without hesitation, the kindly Grandmother Spider shot out a long silver thread and pulled Tallulah and her web-sail in.

Tallulah and Bird Friend told her everything about Buck becoming ill and falling into a deep sleep and how the grey mist had crept into the Meadow silencing everything that lived there. She also told her how she had learned to fly and how she had sailed over the grey mist and through the Old Forest seeking help for her friend.

Grandmother Spider gently caressed her, "Granddaughter, you are very brave to take a journey like that for your friend. I see you have the heart of a Warrior. Warriors always help and take care of those who can't take care of themselves. I have known Buck for many years. He is the Keeper of the Meadow and without him the Meadow will die and all who live there will perish."

When Tallulah heard this she felt a deep sadness and a sense of urgency.

"I will help you Granddaughter," said Grandmother Spider. "But the task will be difficult and challenging. Do you still feel you want to take this journey?" she asked.

Feeling her warrior's heart beating in her chest, Tallulah made her decision.

"Yes," she said. "I will do anything to save my friend and the Meadow."

"There are two tasks you must do," said Grandmother Spider. "Go to the Sacred Mountains that are located on the other side of the Old Forest. Flowing through the mountains you will find the great River of Life. When you get to the River, spin a silver rope of silken threads. Use it to suspend your web-sail between the Spirit World, the Land of Light and Maka Mother Earth. Climb up to the

Spirit World. There you will find a luminescent Red Flower. You must gather some of its pollen and bring it back with you.

When you have finished the first task, spin a silver rope all the way down to the River of Life and gather some of the Ma-hne, the Water of Life, this too you must bring back with you."

Tallulah's eyes were growing large with fear as she thought, *how will I remember all of this?*

Taking a deep breath, she once again found her courage and continued listening very closely to the instructions Grandmother Spider was telling her so she would remember.

"When you have completed both tasks you must take these two powerful healing medicines home with you; when you get back to the Old Barn mix them together. These two, when combined together, become the elixir of light and love, the most powerful of all healing medicines.

Give it to Buck and it will restore him back to health. But you must hurry, for time is running out."

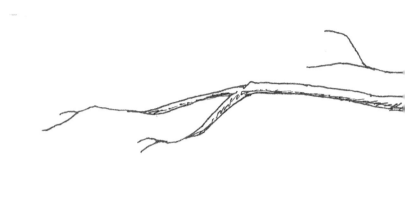

Chapter 5

Up, Up, Up

Behold this day, it is yours to make.

Black Elk, Lakota Holy Man

"I can guide you to the Sacred Mountains, I have been there many times," said Bird Friend.

Waving goodbye and shouting a thank you to Grandmother Spider, they set out right away. With the help of Tate the Wind and Bird Friend guiding her, Tallulah was able to steer her web-sail through the Old Forest to the Sacred Mountains.

The Sacred Mountains were lush emerald green. The clear mountain air had the fragrance of pine trees and the high peaks had clouds around them. Tallulah could feel the strength of the Mountains all around her. Even from a distance she could hear the roaring of the River of Life, and she could smell the clean freshness of its pure water.

She followed the banks of the River until she found a place where the water was calm, flowing gently, and singing a gurgling bubbly song. A bright dancing rainbow hung just over the water. Tallulah knew it was the perfect place between the Spirit World, the Land of Light and Maka Mother Earth to spin her silver rope as Grandmother Spider had instructed her to do.

Tallulah had practiced for long hours spinning and weaving back at the Old Barn, and was a skillful spinner. But this task would take all of her skills to create the silver rope that was needed.

First she asked Bird Friend if he would stay and keep watch over her web-sail until she returned, as she knew this was a journey that she had to take alone. Then she began spinning the silken threads into a silver rope. Up, up, up into the Spirit World of Light. It was a long way up and her legs became shaky. Once she lost her grip and slipped back. But she never stopped until she was all the way to the top.

Pausing a moment to catch her breath and rest her tired

legs, Tallulah saw the luminescent Red Flower, just as Grandmother Spider had said.

She quickly climbed the stalk and jumped into the center of the Flower's blossom. There, on each of its petals she found the shimmery red pollen she needed.

Tallulah said a prayer, thanking the Red Flower for its medicine. That is when she

realized she did not have anything to put the pollen in, so she could take it back with her.

She sat for a moment resting and thinking. Then she thought, *I have eight legs. I can use the hair on two of my legs to gather and hold the pollen.* She gently rubbed two of her legs into the beautiful shimmery red pollen. The pollen stuck to the golden hairs on her long slender legs. Holding her pollen-laden legs close to her body she went back to the silver rope and began her journey back to her web-sail.

Chapter 6

The River

Live as strong as the mountains.

Lakota Warrior

When she arrived back at her web-sail Bird Friend flew aerial somersaults, saying, "You did it. You are so clever and wise."

After resting for a while to regain her strength, Tallulah began spinning the silver rope down to Maka Mother Earth and the River of Life.

Having to hold onto the precious red pollen with two of her legs made it much harder to do her spinning. But she was determined to help her friend Buck and restore life back to the Meadow, so she never stopped weaving.

When she finally reached the calm flowing sky-blue water of the River of Life, she said a prayer thanking Mahne the Spirit of the Water, for its life giving power.

Then she so very carefully stuck out two of her other legs into the rainbow colored mist that rose off the River of Life. Many of the multicolored droplets clung to the golden hairs on her long slender legs. She gently and

carefully pulled her two legs close to her body, so she

would not lose any of the precious droplets.

She quickly climbed back up the silver rope. But with only four legs to climb with it was very difficult. And the red pollen and the water droplets were very heavy to carry.

She said a prayer to the Creator, asking for strength. And she felt the blood of her sacred ancestors running through her. It fully opened her Warrior's heart, giving her the strength she needed to keep climbing. It took a long time but she finally made it back to her web-sail and Bird Friend.

While she rested, with four of her legs folded close to her body, protecting her precious burden, Bird Friend removed the droplets of water that had gathered on the web-sail, anchoring it down.

The day was finished and Wi the Sun had completed his journey across the sky. It was beginning to get dark and the air felt cool and all was silent. The web-sail just hung on the silver rope and they waited.

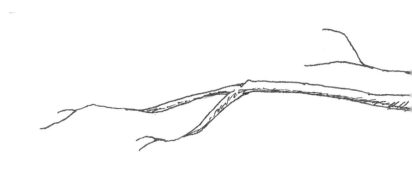

Chapter 7

Friend to the Rescue

All dreams spin out from the same web.

Lakota Elder

Then Hanwi the Moon in her full glory came over the horizon casting her silvery light into the darkness. Tate the Wind blew a soft gentle breath of air. Somewhere between trust and luck, Tallulah released her web-sail from the silver rope and launched it into the night. With magical Bird Friend using the silvery light of the Moon and Wican the Star Nation to navigate with, he quietly guided them through the night on their journey home.

The night with the moon's silvery light was beautiful and magical. Yet it also cast shadows over the land. As they were going back through the Old Forest, Tallulah hugged her legs closer to her body when they saw Owls perched in tree branches. There were many animal sounds. And several times they sailed over yellow eyes shining bright in the bushes.

When at last they came to the Meadow, not even Hanwi the Moon's bright silvery light could penetrate the thick grey mist that covered the ground. The air smelled old and stale; silence was everywhere. The slow creeping mist had almost reached the Old Barn.

Tallulah felt a rush of fear as her heart pounded. Had they arrived in time to save Buck, the Meadow and all who lived there?

Flying above the dark grey mist, they were just a short distance from the Old Barn when out of the corner of her eye Tallulah saw dark shapes flitting toward them. It was a swarm of bats. They began to dive bomb her fragile web-sail. With the bats swarming around her she held tight to her valuable cargo while trying to maneuver her web-sail. She could feel one drop of the precious water beginning to slide off her leg.

Then brave Bird Friend dived, darted, and swooped into the bats holding them off until Tallulah was safe inside the Old Barn, where he joined her. With a sigh of relief, she said, "Thank you" to Bird Friend as she looked anxiously to where Buck still lay in his stall nearly lifeless and barely breathing.

You already possess everything to become great.

Wisdom of the Elders

Tallulah lowered herself on a silken thread into the stall. She took an old leaf that had blown into the barn and rubbed the luminous red pollen off her legs onto the leaf. Then she carefully removed each of the rainbow colored droplets, one by one placing them gently onto the red pollen. Using her long slender legs she mixed them together, creating a shimmering magic elixir.

She dipped her leg into the potion. With the elixir clinging to the golden hairs it took all of her strength to open Buck's lips a tiny slit, just enough for her slender leg to put medicine into his mouth.

She gently stroked his dull mane, while singing an ancient heart song of healing. *"Hey a na ya ho hey, hey a na ya ho hey ya na ya ho hey ya na ya oh hey."* Bird Friend joined her, singing a lovely bird song.

It seemed a long time to Tallulah before she noticed a

shine climbing up the strands of his mane and a gloss

creeping over his dull dry hair. He slowly licked his lips and

opened his eyes like he was waking from a dream. With a

great effort he was able to get to his feet. He stood weakly

with his head hanging down. After standing for a moment

his strength quickly returned. He gave a happy neigh and shook himself all over making his thick shiny mane fall over his eyes.

"Thank you my good friends," he nickered after a moment. "You have saved me from the darkness that was overcoming me."

Tallulah was so happy and filled with joy to see her old friend well again; she jumped up and down on the top board of the stall. Bird Friend flew loops through the rafters of the big Old Barn.

Then he flew back to Tallulah shouting, "You have earned a new name. You are now Tallulah the Flying Spider. Your ancestors would be very proud of you."

A small tear forming in Tallulah's golden eyes made them sparkle. And for a brief moment her white skin blushed pink.

"Thank you my beautiful friend," she happily said with a big smile.

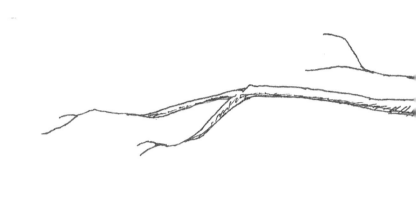

Chapter 9

Gratitude

And the Great Spirit will always be with you.

Native American Wisdom

As Wi the Sun was just peeking over Maka the Earth,

Buck, Tallulah and the magical Bird Friend went outside to

the Meadow. The grey mist was gone and the Meadow was

once again alive with wonderful earthy scents of warm

grass, trees, and

the sweet fragrance of flowers. The songs of nature filled the air.

"I am so grateful to you both for saving my life," said Buck. "But how were you, a small spider, and you the smallest of birds, able to save a big horse like me and restore life to the Meadow?"

Tallulah and Bird Friend smiled at each other. "That my friend," said Tallulah, "Is a skillfully woven story that will entertain us for many evenings to come."

And in this distant magical land that is between up and down and right under our noses, they lived in peace and beauty the rest of their days.

~~ ~~ ~~ ~~ ~~ ~~

But this is not where it ends.

If by chance you are one of the lucky ones who have learned to look past their noses, you may see the magical land between up and down. Look to the sky for a spider in a web-sail accompanied by a tiny bird. You will know it's Tallulah flying off into another great adventure.

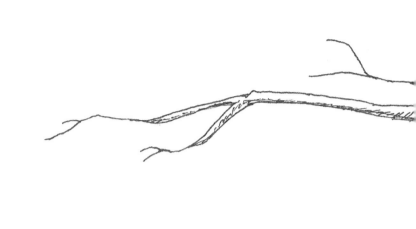

Connect with Gloria

Learn more about Gloria, her latest stories, and

hen she may be storytelling near you by visiting

ww.gloriatwo-feathers.com or connecting with her

line at:

Facebook:

tps://www.facebook.com/gloria.twofeathers

LinkedIn:

tps://www.linkedin.com/in/earthwakeschool

CPSIA information can be obtained
at www.ICGtesting.com
Printed in the USA
FSHW020208210721
83349FS